Infringed

A Journey To The Void

by Aayush Das

Cover Illustration Copyright © 2020 by Aayush Das

Edited by Aayush Das
www.aayushdas.com

Disclaimer

This is a work of fiction. Names, characters, businesses, places, events and incidents are either the products of the author's imagination or used in a fictitious manner. Any resemblance to actual persons, living or dead, or actual events is purely coincidental.

About The Author

Since 1994, the Author has been an undercover member of the fabled Illuminati. He's a skilled master of deception and disguise. He has a day job, he goes to the gym for about twenty days in one calendar year, and he lives in the most inconspicuous country on the planet. The perfect disguise. He lurks in the shadows and secretly works towards his evil agenda of world domination. Like most cunning villains of legend, he is narcissistic. He writes in his free time, stories and novels about the most unworldly things. Like a true escapist, he is lazy and rarely finishes the books that he starts writing. Top secret intelligence reports say that he unwittingly leaves clues about his grand evil plans in his stories and books, but he remains unfazed. In the 21st century world where tons of information flows in all directions all the time, his work may just pass as white noise in the background. The odds against humanity are high. The future looks bleak. Will some hero or heroine step up and shoulder the tumultuous task of reading his mind-numbingly boring work? If at all that happens, humanity just might stand a chance against the evil Author.

Table of Contents

Prologue

"Once upon a time..."

"No daddy, stop."

"What now, Annu?" I tried my best to fake the 'irritated father' look. Her big blue eyes looked back at me curtly, and I at once knew that it was best to not try such tricks. She had her mother's gift of seeing right past my masks. I might as well not wear them.

"How many times have I told you?" She knuckled my shoulder. "Never start a story with 'once upon a time'. It is clichéd and uninteresting."

"I am a scientist, baby girl," I gathered her in my arms and picked her up, "not a writer." Ignoring her whining, I lay her down in her bed and tucked her in. "Besides, it is a bedtime story. It is supposed to make you fall asleep. It is *supposed* to be uninteresting."

"No fair," she protested, kicking about. "It is supposed to be interesting so that I get good dreams."

"Do you want to hear the story or not?"

Yes, the expected sullen face. The ladies in my life knew exactly which buttons to press. But I had developed some immunity to these tactics, thanks to Ananya's mother. Even with the red halo around her pupils, my daughter was beautiful.

"Once upon a time," I kissed my daughter and said, "there was a princess named Humanity. She ruled the great kingdom of Gaia, the mother of all life. The kingdom was paradise, vast and free and teeming with life. The princess bathed in the rivers, drank from streams of sweet water, ate the food mother Gaia presented her with. She scaled the giant snow-capped mountains, dived to the greatest depths of the ocean, and tamed all life as her subjects."

"What happened next?"

"Don't talk, baby girl. Close your eyes. There."

"Humanity believed that Gaia loved her as much as she loved Gaia. But she was naive. She didn't know that Gaia was the force of nature. It could never be tamed and kept in museums. The more powerful our princess became, the more she hurt mother Gaia. She didn't want to. But sometimes we hurt the ones we love the most. The princess didn't realize that in her reign, many of her subjects suffered and died. She was so busy building walls and castles in her kingdom in the name of order that she couldn't notice that the order of nature shook every time she joined two bricks."

"Did she never realize her mistakes?"

"She did. And you should too. If you speak again, I will not finish the story."

"Sorry," she whispered and put her head over my lap. It was warmer than I had expected. No, it was warmer than what I had wanted to expect.

"The princess soon realized that she was hurting mother Gaia. And trust me, she tried to make things right. But sometimes, habits and situations become too powerful for people. The princess had grown accustomed to a lifestyle that flouted the rules of Gaia, and she was unable to undo all the mistakes she had made.

One day, Gaia's unwavering patience finally gave way and she decided to punish the princess for her transgressions. Gaia concluded that it was time for

Humanity to finally step down from the throne and let the kingdom be free and equal again.

But the princess knew this day was coming. She had spent years preparing for the day when Gaia would unleash her wrath and attempt to dethrone her. The princess knew she couldn't resist the power of the great mother nature. Sensing defeat, she packed her bags and ran away from her kingdom, leaving her palaces and fortresses to her subjects who had no use for them. Princess Humanity left her kingdom a poor little girl with no means of surviving in the big bad world. But she had hope. She had found another kingdom far away from home and had readily decided to conquer it and continue her life as a princess again.

But when she reached her newfound kingdom, she found that it was nothing like the paradise she had once ruled!"

I felt wetness on my cheeks as my little princess snuggled with me for comfort. Her hot breath washed over my hands caressing her tiny face. I took her shivering hands in my own, and at that moment I knew that I would never get to tell her the end of the story.

The Infection

Not many people attended her funeral.

My daughter died and the world didn't care for it. It would be wrong to call this place the world, though. This was two per cent of the fragment of the real world that had made the jump. And that fragment had been 0.01 per cent of the total population of humanity plus supplies. After seven years at Infringe, I had forgotten what the term 'world' meant.

I looked to the sky - purple, with dense smoky clouds that moved with unimaginable speed in the higher atmosphere. Eternal dusk hung around our settlement. Maybe it's my daughter's death that makes me talk so negatively. You could call it eternal dawn if you wish. Whichever way you look at it, dawn or dusk, it is eternal.

She was supposed to die at any cost. This world was not meant for her. She was a sweet little thing, meant for a different world. Not the mess called Infringe.

"It's best we incinerate her," Clarice had said to me, "since the ground is already rotting with corpses."

So I took little Annu to the crescent hillside, mounted on a wooden sledge, and pushed her off the top whilst staying behind the shadow. I couldn't see her as she slid down the sun-facing side of the hill. But I could hear the fizz as her delicate skin melted against the bright of the day, the prick as her bones fried, the crackle as her remains caught fire. And I had no way to say goodbye one last time. She had been lost, even before I let Infringe set her on fire.

Things hadn't changed much in the past twenty years. Many fathers had lost their children, many husbands their wives, and vice versa. Our new world had given us diseases that we had never seen or heard of before, and the fact that most of our fellow settlers had died even before we set foot on the planet didn't help.

"We are in grave danger," the EarthGov President had announced on 1900 hours GMT on 25 December 2756, "but I am glad to tell you that most of us will come out of it alive if we adhere to the following procedure. The novel strain of Thanatos virus has been isolated, and while no cure or vaccine yet exists we expect to come up with a solution soon. However, we need you to comply with government regulations. Together, we will beat this virus."

That was when Scrutiny began. We were asked to report for medical check-ups, blood tests, psychological evaluations, and our profiles were sent to the government for review. The ones who were deemed 'Infected' by the evaluating AI were sent to Geneva where hope waited for us, or so they said. The rest of the human population was sent to several camps all over the world for further Scrutiny. They were told they would be safe there. Safe from the infectious outbreak of a novel respiratory disease-causing virus that was apparently powerful enough to wipe humanity off the face of the Earth.

"Infected," my report had read, and I was taken away from my family by soldiers dressed in biohazard suits while the people of my neighbourhood hid in their houses and closed the doors and windows. My wife and daughter were taken away too, them having been in contact with me.

I faintly remember begging the soldiers to let my daughter go. They had simply ignored me. There was no telling how they would 'dispose of' the Infected. I dreaded whatever they had in mind, but part of me knew that it was morally wrong to ask for her freedom. Humanity was at stake and we were going to be collateral damage.

"Hello ladies and gentlemen," we were finally crammed together in a large facility called Project Thanatos. All of us knew that the new virus that had put the world into this chaos had been named Thanatos. "We are terribly sorry for the inconvenience you have been put through in the past few days. We thank you for putting up with us so far. Today, we will debrief you about your situation and about Project Thanatos. We assure you, if you follow procedure, you will go out of this facility safe and sound."

I was sure it was all a lie. Some soothing words to calm down the chicken before slaughter. They had no plans of curing us, that was certain. In the seven days they had kept me and my family hostage, I hadn't seen even the most basic hygiene and sanitation measures being properly taken. I was the seventh person who was sent in for 'debriefing', and I prayed that they drugged me and finished me off in my sleep at least.

"Welcome, Dr Naik," a female voice escorted me. "I expect your stay here has not been very comfortable so far. I apologize for that. Please have a seat."

"Listen," I said. "I have a wife and a baby daughter. Whatever you do to me, at least treat them like you would treat your own family. I will beg for it."

The lady had looked at me through her bobbed hair. She couldn't help but smirk. "We're not going to kill you, Dr Naik. We're not going to kill anyone."

"What do you mean?" I was dazed. "Then why did you round us all up? And what are you going to do about the infection?"

"That is what I am here to tell you," she said. "There is no infection. There is no novel virus."

I slumped into the chair behind me, aghast.

"What do you mean? No infection?"

My mind couldn't process the situation I was in. Only one question remained in my mind.

"What the hell is Project Thanatos?"

Project Thanatos

I was in what appeared to be a police precinct interrogation-room. A single fluorescent light above my head, a double-glass window through which someone was definitely watching my 'briefing', and the woman sitting across the excessively large table.

"What is going on here?" I asked.

"Do you mind if I smoke?" She produced a Marlboro from her coat and put it between her teeth.

I signalled her to not mind me.

"You want some too?" She said after lighting the cigarette and taking a satisfying puff.

"No thanks."

Her lips were well painted with deep red lipstick but her fingers conveyed that she was a chain smoker.

"You know that stuff can kill you, right?" I said.

She looked at me with a flirtatious grin and said, "I wish someone had told me this ten years ago."

I thought it was best to let her smoke in peace, so I sat back and watched her burn down the cigarette. When she was done, she crushed the red stub against the polished silver table. It left a distinct mark.

"Okay now," I asked again, "tell me what is going on here?"

She got up and approached me. When she was close enough, she bent until her face was at level with mine.

"Tell me," she asked, "what are the craziest apocalypse theories you have ever read?"

A catalogue opened up in my mind as I tried to recall all those crazy end-of-the-world theories I had ever read about. Zombie outbreak, a deadly virus, intelligent robots realizing that mankind was redundant, getting hit by a comet...

"Why do you ask me that?"

"Listen to this."

She waved towards the window, signalling whoever was outside to play an audio recording.

**** As technology progressed it got smaller and smaller. Pretty soon we entered the realms of Nanotechnology. Nanobots. They were microscopic robots designed to do all sorts of tasks, mostly in the medical field where they could seek out and eradicate bacterial infections, repair tissue damage, mend blood vessels. Lots of things that would be very helpful to everyone.*

They had the ability to rearrange single atoms and for instance, make water out of minerals and sand. They were able to take carbon atoms and turn them in diamonds. They could pick up raw materials and rearrange them into what they needed.

*Obviously they were extremely difficult to make, being microscopic. Scientists realized the only way to make them would be to use the Nanobots themselves. To make them self replicating. So each one was a microscopic Nanobot factory. ****

A glass of water was kept before me, which startled me since I had not noticed anyone entering or leaving the room, and the audio continued.

****But there was a danger. What would happen if just one of them were accidentally thrown away? The misplaced nanobot would pretty much go around changing atoms into robots. Then those robots would make more, and more, and more, at an exponential rate until the horror unfolded. Scientists believe within 72 hours every single atom on earth could be turned into a Nanobot. All buildings, cars, plants, rocks, the water, animals and yes, even us humans... ****

"That is how we are going to end," the woman said, placing herself on the table. "To tackle nanobot rampancy, we had used genetic coding from toads and fish, to ensure that nanobots had limited self-replication and a small time-window over which they would work. After that, they'd go dead or dormant.

But we didn't understand how nature works. Scientists say that it happened because we didn't factor the fact that animals have limited lifespans. That is why their reproduction capabilities are limited. But if an animal cell becomes immortal, it would have no restrictions to self replicate as much as possible."

"What do you mean?"

"It was hundreds of years ago," she said, "when nanotech came into force. We used them everywhere, renovated everything we wanted. We recreated the animals that had gone extinct, created fancy new species as per our imagination, made whatever we wanted into whatever we wanted. We basically tamed nature."

"And we were wrong?"

"Yes, we were."

A video played out in front of me on a holo panel while the woman continued talking.

"We forgot about evolution," she said. "We forgot to realize that as soon as something becomes sentient, it gets the power to evolve, change its genetic code.

Our nanobots evolved too. It was a slow process, pretty undetectable, natural. The nanobots were our creation but they were, after all, coded with animal genes."

"And an animal will compete with the other animals to extend its lineage and pass on its genetic code as many times as possible," I sighed in horror. "Nanobots going rampant was always inevitable."

The holo panel vanished and the room suddenly felt suffocating. The truth dawned upon me. We had been damned all this time and we never noticed.

"How much time do we have?" I asked her.

"Three days from now," she said, "the Osaka nanobot facility will be the point of origin of the rampancy. The scientists were quick enough to alert us ten years ago, when they noticed the coding variations in their nanobots. once the rampancy begins, it will take about seventy-two hours until it spreads all over the Earth."

I buried my head in my hands. The room felt dark and terrorizing.

"How could they predict all this ten years ago?" I asked, aghast. "And if they could, why didn't they destroy all the nanobots altogether."

"Because the nanobots were everywhere by then. They were used for almost everything. And there was no way we could track down and destroy every single one of them. Not that we didn't try.

As for the prediction, the first nanobot was created in the Osaka research facility. It was replicated and used to create new nanobots. Then the newer bots took over and the alpha, the first nanobot ever, was kept in their lab for observation. After centuries of research, it was found that the alpha was evolving. The next step was to determine when it would evolve enough to become rampant."

I shrugged. At that point, that was all I could do.

"But don't you worry," I felt a hand upon my shoulder. "You will not die with this planet. This is the part where Project Thanatos comes in."

"What do you mean?"

"We had ten years to prepare for this," she said. "We weren't just sitting idly by. We spent the time to devise an escape plan. Not for all of us, that wasn't possible. But we can save just about enough of mankind to carry on. Seven hundred thousand of us."

"How do you plan on doing that?"

"This facility," she said. "This Project Thanatos facility is what we came up with."

"You mean we will stay safe inside this thing?"

She threw her head back and laughed at my question.

"In a way," she said, "yes."

My questioning glance prodded her to speak further.

"Okay, so this is the thing. There is nothing in the known universe that can save us from nanobot rampancy here on Earth. So we looked to the stars and found a new home for you people. This is what this facility is about. It is a spaceship designed to take you all to a new planet."

Unsettling Questions

"You are crazy!"

The woman briefing me had no regard for my taunt, naturally, so it was up to me to proceed with my counter-question.

"Assembling seven-hundred thousand people under one roof is one thing," I said, "but how do you plan on sending all of us into space? Hell, how would you even achieve lift-off with a payload this big? And how do you plan on telling your plan to all of us within three days?"

"You ask the strangest questions, Dr Naik," she sighed. "Why, the briefing procedure has already been finished."

I fisted the table in front of me and stood up indignantly.

"What are you saying? You've only briefed six people. I am the seventh."

The woman approached me with a steeled gaze, putting a gentle yet firm hand on my shoulder.

"There there," she said, "relax. There is no need to raise voices in small rooms like this."

That was when I realized that she was more serious than me. I let her sit me down and explain.

"See for yourself," she guided my eyes towards the other end of the table, where a holo panel appeared. In it, I saw the images from the time my briefing had been going on. A matrix of chairs had been placed in the meeting hall. They were all occupied by people who had their hands and legs strapped to the chairs. The peculiar part was the headgear. I instantly recognized those as the virtual sim headgear that was used for archaic virtual reality games in the twenty-first century.

The fool had been me all along. I should've realized that these people were more than resourceful. They couldn't use memory-injection, given that it utilized nanobots, but they could very well pick up archaic technology and use it differently.

"And what makes me so different?"

"You," she echoed, "Dr Naik, and the other six people I briefed, are going to help all these people survive out there in the new world that you find. These are people of the Nanotech Age, they have no idea how to survive without the aid of the technology they're used to."

She turned to face me, her pen pointed towards my teeth.

"You, however, are a scientist. And a reverse-engineering specialist at that. There is nobody who could better teach those people how to learn to live without something else doing all the heavy lifting for them."

"And who are the other six?"

"Oh, don't be so impatient," she smiled. "You'll meet them soon enough. What matters right now is whether you're up for the task or not, Dr Naik!"

The question was more difficult than I had thought it'd be. I had my own family to take care of. Besides, leadership had never been my cup of tea.

"Why don't you take the job?" I drove my point home, at last. "You brought us this far, it is best that you lead us through to the very end."

She went quiet.

"Why won't you?"

"I wish I could," she said. "But I am not going to make this trip with you. So, you see, I am in no position to lead your pack. It has to be someone from your side."

"What are you talking about?" Sentiment had found its way up to my throat. "You arranged all of this, didn't you? Then why are you not coming?"

She coldly produced another cigarette from her coat. This time she didn't stick it in her lips. She held it between her stubby fingers and tore it in half, letting the nicotine fall on the floor below.

"Lung cancer," she sighed, "final stage. My doctor told me I will die within the next two years. That was two years ago."

I thought the pause was meant for me to register the impact of what she had just told me, but it turned out to be a routine one.

"That was when I was hired for this. All the personnel that work in this facility are terminally ill. We're all dead men and women. And that is why the government entrusted the biggest secret in the world to us. This project."

"Now," she declared, "if we have all that sorted out, shall we move on to the part where I tell you what you have to do?"

I nodded, letting her lead me away. She took me out of the room, into the gathering chamber where we had all assembled the first time we were brought to Project Thanatos, and showed me around the marvellous structures of the installation. The most important part of the construction, she maintained, was the fact that it was all zero per cent nanotech.

She told me that since we had no proper technology available to us, the best we had was over a thousand years old (back when we could see our machines working with the naked eye), terraforming was out of the question. So was a space-station. These were obvious solutions, and pointless, since both of these would depend on Earth and its resources which were now beyond saving.

So, the only logical option we had to our disposal was to find a rock in space that had just the right temperature, the correct gravity, atmosphere, liquid water...basically another Earth, and hijack it. The plan sounded so far so good to me. Only one thing bothered my mind.

How were we going to take Project Thanatos into space? The damn thing wasn't even shaped like a rocket.

"The facility doesn't need to go anywhere," she answered my doubts. "We will drop it in hyperspace, relativity will do the rest. The relevant course and calculations are already fed into the servers."

Hyperspace. Another fancy move my magician had rolled up in her sleeve. The 'shortcut' pathways in spacetime accessible by phenomena called wormholes.

Again. One issue stood. There was no existing technology to open up a wormhole. The energy requirement was too high. Unless...

"You are thinking correctly," she said grimly, contemplating on the shock on my face. "We're going to blow up the Earth."

Ultimate Sacrifice

"All cargo loaded, ma'am," a voice crackled over the radio. "The Project is a go!"

Cargo meant about seven hundred thousand people, in hypersleep, and useful material and equipment we would need when we went to start settling a new planet.

"We'll stay tight on schedule, then," the woman leading me instructed. "When is the lift-off?"

"T-minus six hours."

That meant we could spare a supper, she said. I said I could use the last meal at home. I was led outside the Project Thanatos facility, where I saw several encampments already in place.

"These are for me and my crew," she told me. "Front-row tickets to the end of the world."

"This is a stupid plan," I said. "The bad thing is that you've already gone through with it."

"I think it is a brilliant plan. Turning into nanobots is not the way I'd like to die."

"No, you'd rather go down in an explosion."

An explosion would be an understatement for what we were going to do to the Earth. The plan was to propel Project Thanatos into hyperspace, and we were going to use Earth as the fuel to achieve the energy required for the feat. After about six hours, that would be done by pumping up antimatter into the Earth's core. The resulting explosion would destroy one half of the Earth and hurl away chunks of the other half into space. Our facility, then, would fall *inside* the freshly created wormhole. Our ship's transmitters were set to vibrate at a frequency that would be same as the natural frequency of the wormhole about to be created.

"How will we stand the massive force?"

"The ship will not experience any forces. If anything, it will experience a loss of forces acting upon it. It will be as if someone swiped the carpet off from under your feet."

"You interviewed seven people," I asked. "When do I meet the other six?"

"You will meet them inside the ship," she said, "once you set sail. Each one of you will be in charge of one hundred thousand people." She tagged me on my left wrist with a microchip implant device. "This implant contains all of the information of your lot. If anything happens to any of them, you get notified."

The implant instantly ran a health and biometrics diagnostics and returned an 'All-Clear'. It included my wife and child too. I could monitor anyone I wanted, anywhere I wanted, anytime I wanted.

"Hyperspace is anomalous space," the woman told me. "The laws of physics hold differently there. And all we know about it, we have already programmed into the ship. Once you get inside the wormhole, the seven of you shall meet at the bridge. You may not like each other very much, but you have to keep each other alive. So play along."

"What will happen to the rest of humanity? I mean, not all humans live on Earth. We have so many space stations. There are several million up there. What are we going to do about them?"

"They won't survive without Earth to support them, supply them, help them navigate and stay in orbit around their respective planets."

"Do they even know what is going to happen?"

"No," the reply was cold and remorseless, "nobody knows. Nobody could know, or this plan would fail even before it began."

We spoke nothing for a while. In the shadows, we had discussed the plan to slit billions of throats in a matter of minutes. And given another chance, I'd have done it again. Any man would. Saving humanity was of primary importance here, and my family was in the circle of safety. That was all I needed to consider.

"What is your name?" I finally asked. "I never got your name."

"My name, Dr Naik," she smiled, "is of absolutely no consequence."

Two hours left. All parts of the ship had been sealed. I was inside the dormitory area, the place where all the hypersleep chambers were kept. Hypersleep was a good way to pass the time, except that time didn't really pass for one in that state. The cells would remain frozen in the same state. When thawed, the person wouldn't be one second older. This was a safe bet for anomalous situations like a hyperspace jump, during which space and time could both behave rather oddly.

I was supposed to jump into one of those pods too. As soon as we were safely inside hyperspace, I'd be thawed and summoned to the bridge. When we reached our destination, these pods would separate from the main ship and land on the planet. The ship would dock itself in the planet's orbit and act as a survey satellite capable of sending and receiving payloads from the surface.

I had been told that it was unlikely that we would be able to send a payload in the first twenty years. We had a lot of development to do once we got there, and we'd have to do it from scratch.

"Everything good in there?" The woman's voice broke in over my communication channel.

"Looks fine to me," I said. "You people surely collected a whole lot of junk to make this thing."

There was laughter on the other side.

"Yes," she said, "this is all we could get for you. Take it or throw yourself away."

I opened my pod. The inside was a bubbly, cushioned surface that had a strange green glow. The outer screens displayed the vitals and biometrics while the inner display showed up the date, time and other relevant data that might be of importance to the person going in.

"Activate outer cameras of the ship," I instructed Des Cartes, the AI on Project Thanatos. "I am going to hypersleep, but I want to see whatever happened when I wake up."

I was asleep when the world ended. Billions of people died, probably vanished without a trace, in a matter of seconds. It was a single burst of antimatter that was sent to the core. The Earth shook, riled up a little, and then, without warning, a large part of it was gone. Simply ceased to exist. The rest was fired away and might be speeding through space as what you'd identify as asteroids or comets.

So that's how the Earth died. We found out that it was going to die and take us all with it. But we weren't ready to die yet. So we killed it with our own hands instead.

Obliteration Imminent

"Play footage," I was surprised at the coarseness of my voice, probably a result of the quick thaw.

"The images you are about to see," Des Cartes replied, "might be disturbing and emotionally unsettling to you. It is recommended that you refrain from watching this for some time."

"I understand," I said, "but I need to see this. Right now."

"As you wish."

The footage was about five minutes in length. It was the record of the first hyperspace jump humanity had made, at the cost of Earth. It hadn't taken much. First, we pumped antimatter into the Earth's core. The resulting reaction readily converted most of our planet into energy, as I could see on the video. There were strange lights emanating in all directions. One side of Earth had been split open, like a deep gash of light. Several other pores opened up across the surface, and our planet soon looked like a giant disco ball.

Then, without warning, a strong gust of energy took apart whatever was left of Earth. There wasn't much to take apart, though, only the thin crust had remained. When that was gone too, all that remained was Project Thanatos, and a rip in space-time where the Earth had once been.

"What is the current status of the solar system?" I asked.

"It is hard to determine with the current parameters I have," Des Cartes said. The AI had no unessential subroutines, so it was pretty no-nonsense and straight to the point. "I don't think it matters, though. There isn't any life there that would be affected."

Life? Of course not. We had made sure to leave nothing living whenever we left a place. It had been our tradition for as long as history could remember.

"Where are the others?" I asked as soon as I remembered.

"The Captains will join you on the bridge shortly," the AI's digitized voice cracked over. "The passengers are in hypersleep. They will stay that way during the course of the journey."

"Where are we going?"

Des Cartes hesitated. That would probably be an inaccurate, even unjust, thing to say. Given the fact that Des Cartes was monitoring and controlling almost every subsystem on the ship, and it was doing it all in the background, it was blasphemy to assume that a human asking questions should even expect answers. And yet Des Cartes answered, unfailingly, every time.

It opened a holo panel in front of me. The panel displayed our current navigation route through hyperspace and the terminal point where it was supposed to open. The said exit was a solar system in the Vega constellation. And guess what, it was again the third planet in the system that we had chosen to inhabit.

"Tobias-33738," Des Cartes announced, "code name Infringe."

The displayed image was beautiful as if Earth's long lost sister was looking back at us. The planet was blue, with green and brown continents on the surface. The surface had more water than land, another striking likeness with our own planet.

"Beautiful, isn't it?"

I could say that I wasn't startled by the voice that crept up from behind me, but that would be a pathetic attempt at lying. I spun by my heels faster than my mind could register the question, only to come face to face with a woman with the most amazing green eyes.

"Hello," she extended her hand to me, "I am Clarice. Clarice von Goethe. You must be another Captain."

"Dr Hrishikesh Naik," I shook her hand with a smile. "You can call me Dr Naik."

"Yes, that would be very kind," she chuckled. "Your first name is quite a mouthful, Doctor. Are you a medic, if you don't mind me asking?"

"Oh, no, not that. I am a scientist. A reverse-engineer and a keen environmentalist."

"And I would assume you are the one who's in charge of the *other* lot."

The new voice that joined the conversation was very deep, very stable. It was the kind of voice that was best suited to narrate a story, a voice that was strong and unflinching like a mountain.

"What do you mean by the *other* lot?" I mimicked. Even though the voice was impressive, the tone wasn't. As I turned, I was faced by an old man who appeared old by no means, except his silver hair and moustache. He had strong features, muscular body, and a face that seemed to be bent in scorn against the degrading morals of the society. This could be a typical conservative old man, except that he wasn't.

"You know son," he said, "the blacks and the whatnot. The other lot."

Clarice von Goethe wasn't quite amused by his demeanour. Racism had long been declared illegal, yet it had never really died. It flourished like every social evil in the world did, sometimes behind the curtains, sometimes too overt for comfort.

"I am not black," I declared. "I am an Indian."

"You're black enough for me."

"Actually, where I come from, this complexion is called 'wheatish'. And trust me, for someone who seems to have such an agenda against black people, your knowledge about the colour seems a little shaky."

"I think we should not waste our time with cultural and social differences," Clarice von Goethe cut in. "We lost a planet today, seven billion people with it. Now let us get all these people, and ourselves, to Infringe. There, we could all go our separate ways. Is that okay with you, Mister..."

"Ezekiel," the man took her hand and kissed it. "Frederick Ezekiel."

We spent an hour discussing the future of Infringe. We were joined by the other Captains too - Mohammad Arif Hussain of the Middle East, Zlatin Ivanovich from Russia, Amelia Brahe from Denmark, and Eikichi Shigemitsu from Japan. During the course of the discussion, I soon learned that these people weren't meant to just take Project Thanatos safely home. In fact, that didn't seem to be their purpose at all. Instead, it seemed that these people were more concerned about getting political power once we reached Infringe. I started feeling out of place, a feeling that I saw on the faces of Clarice von Goethe and Frederick Ezekiel as well.

"Alert," Des Cartes cut short the discussion that was slowly heating up. "We have a code red threat."

"What is it, Des Cartes?" Frederick's voice tore through the abrupt silence.

"We are approaching the hyperspace rift we are supposed to jump out of," it said. "But the rift is not as big as we had calculated. It seems that attenuation at the Earth terminal end over time has shrunk the wormhole."

"Can the ship go through the wormhole?" Ivanovich asked.

"It is possible," said Des Cartes, "but the wormhole is shrinking fast and it is very difficult to make a smooth exit. Besides, if any of the walls of the ship touch the event horizon, the damage to the ship will be extensive."

"Give me the odds, Des Cartes," I asked. "What are the chances that none of us dies if we go as planned and take the ship through the shrinking wormhole."

"I could give you a larger number," Des Cartes answered, "if you ask me the odds that *all* of you die."

Last Hope, Lost Hope

"It seems," Ivanovich remarked, "jumping inside hyperspace was only half of the solution. Getting out was the other half of it."

We were the last of humanity, aboard one ship that was hurtling at unimaginable speeds through anomalous space, and we were on a collision course with the folds of space-time.

"We cannot resign ourselves to luck," Clarice von Goethe said. "We have to find another way out."

"I so agree with you, Miss," Ivanovich replied, "but I don't see many options in front of us."

Eikichi seemed to be busy in his own thoughts. He seemed uncomfortable, irritated even. He let the arguments pile up at the table, and then broke in without warning.

"What if we abandon ship?"

It had been the first idea in my mind too, but I had rubbished it off almost instantly. The plan had been to keep Project Thanatos in orbit around Infringe so that it could provide us geological and meteorological data. Without it, we would be sitting ducks on the unknown planet. But in the current situation, I realized that being sitting ducks would be far batter than being dead ducks.

"We could take the escape pods," I found myself adding to Eikichi's idea, "fill them up with as many resources as possible. Once planet-side, we could meet up and pool the resources. Des Cartes can plot the approach courses for all the pods."

"Doing that from here could be risky," Des Cartes warned. "Whatever data I have on Infringe is outdated, since the planet is about twenty million light-years from Earth."

"You mean your data is off by twenty goddamn million years?" Frederick Ezekiel had successfully struck panic in our camp.

"Its Physics," I declared, "none of us can do anything about it. If someone looked at our planet from Infringe right now, they'd probably see dinosaurs."

"Yes," Ivanovich said, "and if they reach Earth they'll realize that there is no Earth at all."

"There is no need to panic," Des Cartes came to my aid. "Infringe lies in a very stable solar system of the Spiral Galaxy. When I say my data is off, it means that my data about the planet's current geological state is not accurate. But the planet is there, and it is very much inhabitable. We have kept a close eye on the planet."

"But how could you? Even light takes twenty million years to travel between Infringe and our telescopes."

"You are currently in a giant spaceship which is going to cover the journey between Earth and Infringe in about five solar days," Des Cartes explained. "Do you think we would have trouble sending radio waves to Infringe? Or photons for that matter."

Applause would be very fitting in the situation. Des Cartes had defused the tension on the bridge very tactfully, although it was queer that it didn't come up with the idea on its own.

"You did mention that it is risky," I observed. "What risks were you talking about?"

"I have to launch the pods randomly towards the planet," came the reply. "But I am afraid some pods may land in areas where the inmates wouldn't be able to survive. I have no means to chart a proper safe course for all pods until we get close enough to the planet. The plan was to keep Project Thanatos with all the passengers in orbit for three days, observing the planet. Then we would launch the pods. If I launch them from here, we risk lives."

"Give us numbers, Des Cartes," my voice went cold. "How many lives?"

"As many as two per cent of the passengers could die if I launch the pods from here."

The percentage was a tough figure to refer to while making moral calls like this. Two per cent of seven hundred thousand people were around fourteen thousand people. If we made the call, we risked fourteen thousand lives. But then, we had just murdered seven billion people who had no idea of what was going on.

"That two per cent could include all seven of us," Eikichi said. "We don't condemn others on our behalf, at least. Everybody gets a fair chance. This is the only way."

"If we are making this decision," Clarice said grimly, "it must be unanimous. If anyone objects this decision, now is the time to speak."

All seven of us hoped someone would object, but none of us did. The motion was passed. And hence, we decided to bid farewell to Project Thanatos and carry on with our journey.

I made my way through the hive of pods until I reached CZ-47, the pod where my wife and child were sleeping. I waited for Des Cartes to open it and fill it with food rations using the conveyor bots until the pod was at full capacity minus one person. I entered then, my fingertips running across the hatch inside which my wife slept, waking her up like I had done all these years.

By the time she woke up from hypersleep, we had already jettisoned off the ship. I told her everything that had happened in the past several days, obliteration of the Earth, the seven captains of the ship we had just abandoned, the danger looming over us, and the risk we had all taken.

"It is just a phase," she said. "Good things and bad things have one thing in common. They both happen in bunches."

"Event horizon approaching," Des Cartes announced on the comms line. "Please remain calm."

I had no idea why would Des Cartes make such an announcement when everybody was in hypersleep. I reckoned that the announcement was made exclusively for my pod.

"There it is," my wife said, "Infringe."

I naturally turned to look at the planet I was about to colonize. The sight was majestic for a moment, but only for a moment, and then the bitter taste of reality shook me inside out.

"Activate manual control," I commanded, "right now."

"What's wrong?" My wife held me by the arm while the system handed over control of the pod to me.

"Look at the planet closely," I said. "What do you see?"

She looked through the polarizing window, gawking more than looking until she realized it too.

"What is going on here?"

"Nothing fancy," I said. "It is doing the same thing around its star that our moon used to do around us. Its planetary rotation is synchronized with its orbit around its star. It's tidally locked in its orbit around this red giant."

"So, you mean that one side of the planet always faces the star?"

I nodded. "And one side always faces away. By the looks of it, the dayside should be around seven to eight hundred degrees Celsius, while the night side is minus hundred-odd."

Her hand slipped from my arm and dropped to her thigh.

"Des Cartes," I said, "this planet is not what we were expecting it to be. There is no hope here. We need to abort the mission."

The communication line was silent.

"Des Cartes," I shouted into the receiver, "DES CARTES, ANSWER ME GODDAMN IT..."

Infringe

I dipped the bucket into the icy cold water, trying my best to keep my fingers away from the water. More than one person had lost their fingers to frostbite fetching water from these shores.

Once the bucket was full, I'd take it to the warm side and put it near the ridge. It would take a few minutes until the water was suitably warm and ready to use.

It had been three years since we landed on Infringe, three years since the futility of our survival plan had dawned upon me. I remembered it all, clear as day.

"What are you going to do now?" My wife was hysterical. "We cannot land on Infringe, we cannot stay up here, and we cannot contact Des Cartes."

The same questions had been pestering me. The pods were not meant to stay in orbit. They'd all eventually land, even if we tried to avoid landing. Infringe was a prison of ice and fire, it was simply not possible to colonize that planet. Maybe, with better equipment and preparation, we could terraform the planet and make it habitable. But if we had that sort of option, we'd not come so far into deep space. We could very well live on Titan, Mars, or Venus.

But terraforming was not possible in our current circumstances. The best of our technology depended on nanotech, and nanotech was the peril that had forced us to escape in the first place. We had no option but to find out a planet that could give us Earth-like conditions. We had chosen Infringe for the same. And we had been wrong.

"One side of the planet always faces the star," I said, "and one side always faces away. Both are desolate, uninhabitable places and we can't land there."

"But there is a sweet spot on the planet," I continued. "The planet's twilight line. There is this tiny region between the dayside and the night side where the temperature is just fine. It's not much, just a few kilometres wide, but it is there. We can land there."

"Are you sure?"

"I wouldn't risk our daughter's life on a maybe."

And I had landed my pod on the small patch on Infringe where there was neither day nor night. When I stepped out of my pod, I could see the others cruising far away into the dayside or veering towards the night side. They were all landing in a death-trap, while I and my wife watched them helplessly from safety.

"Dr Hrishikesh," an automated voice blared from my life pod, filling me with rage. It was Des Cartes.

"I am so sorry, Doctor," it said. "I temporarily shut myself down when we crossed the event horizon. The region was filled with electromagnetic noise which could be detrimental to my system. I rebooted just now."

"We don't have time for small talk," I said hoarsely. "Redirect all remaining life pods to this area I've mapped on my nav-computer. Do it quick."

"I already have. I run a quick system diagnostics after I rebooted and in the process found out what the problem with Infringe is."

"Those who have landed on the dayside and the night side," I asked, "can we save them?"

"I'm afraid that's not possible," Des Cartes replied. "Most of those pods have already been opened by their crew, who would be deceased by now."

"What about the ones who haven't?"

"Even if they stay inside," Des Cartes said, "they don't have water and rations. They will die out in a week or two. If they go to hypersleep again, however, the ones on the dayside may last a year or so. The pods on the dayside will not run out of power, but unchecked contamination of bodily fluids will kill the inhabitants. The ones on the night side, though, will be out of power within a month."

"So, you mean they cannot be saved?"

For the first time, Des Cartes answered a question with silence.

"How many?" I asked Des Cartes later that day.

"Fourteen thousand one hundred and seven people. Eighty-four per cent of them, male."

Fourteen thousand. I remembered that number. It was two per cent of the number of people who had boarded

Project Thanatos. It was the number of people we had expected to lose during our landing on Infringe.

But things turned out quite differently, and fourteen thousand people survived. The remaining six hundred eighty-six thousand, ninety-eight per cent of our colony, had been lost beyond redemption.

"How many of the captains have survived?"

"Three, including you. Miss Clarice von Goethe and Reverend Frederick Ezekiel survived the trip."

"How fast can you probe the livable area on this planet?"

"Three days."

"Send the probes now, then," I commanded. "Light a beacon and instruct all those who remain to gather here. We need to sit down and plan our strategy very carefully from here. Survival on this planet will take a lot more than conventional farming until we become advanced enough."

"Yes, Doctor."

"And Des Cartes, seal all the life pods. The resources we have aboard them need to be used wisely."

"Okay Doctor," Des Cartes said. "It's done."

My wife looked at me with a glint of terror. I held her hand, but I knew the same terror was there in my eyes too. If there was someplace called hell, I could bet it drew inspiration from the planet we had run off to. One side of the planet was a fiery realm which would incinerate anyone who set foot there within seconds, while the other side was a frozen, icy world where life would not dare to go. In between was a tiny speck of land, three-kilometre wide, where we had set camp. There was freshwater towards the area that merged into the night side. The soil seemed fertile enough too.

But we had found no signs of native life on the planet's most (probably the only) habitable zone. Whatever that once lived on the planet had gone extinct long ago, it seemed. I don't believe in omens, but I did that day. And I could see that they were not in our favour.

If I went by the facts and their implied indications, I would say that Infringe was not capable of providing us anything. Anything except death.

I felt my wife at my side, holding on to me. She had watched me noiselessly, contemplating the depths of my fear. I felt her lips press against my cheek.

"We are still alive," she said. "Don't give up just yet."

Faith

"You know what our biggest problem is?

No, it's not stupidity. We could, instead, be too intelligent for our own good. Like we were when we systematically "outsmarted" mother nature and embarked upon a great journey that led us to Infringe.

It isn't some ideological defect or intellectual deficiency either. No, we are more than well-endowed in those departments.

Our biggest problem is forgetfulness."

My wife had laughed at my statement, followed by our daughter. It wasn't every day that I got philosophical, and this kind of reaction happened whenever I did. My wife disagreed with me on most things, and she had followed the trend on this one as well. She had said, in her loveliest tone, that it wasn't our short-lived memory that caused us trouble.

"It is a lack of faith."

I could agree with her. Over the course of seven years, we had lost faith in our plan to rule Infringe, like we once did Earth. We had soon given up the idea of ruling and accepted the rules this planet had imposed upon us. The people had forgotten the original plan, the life pods that had brought us on this desolate world now lay abandoned, Des Cartes was long forgotten, and the captains were not leaders anymore. Frederick Ezekiel somewhat performed his duties as a captain, though. His religion had become the only religion practised on Infringe.

Clarice von Goethe had turned over to keeping the people from each other's throats. She spent her days trying to find a cure to the black fever, the deadly disease that had found us on Infringe. It was the same disease that killed my wife, and then my daughter. While Ezekiel had become the voice of God on our planet, von Goethe had become the watchful protector of our people and their laws.

And I had reduced myself to a reclusive, antisocial scientist who was rarely seen outside his hut.

But then, was it the lack of faith? Or was it because we had all forgotten who we were really supposed to be?

"You are wasting away your life like this," I had often been told. "Get back to society, become a responsible member of it. Find another bride for yourself, be happy. But don't be useless."

"To hell with them," I thought. What society were they hoping to build on a planet where it was always six o clock? There was nothing to explore, everywhere looked the same, and the places that were worth exploring were inaccessible.

Farming had worked, at least, and we were sustainable in the current state. But once our population size grew, we would have nowhere to go. The only water resource was a freshwater sea, towards the night side, that froze away within a couple of kilometres from the shore. And that ice wasn't going to melt, so we were going to run out of water sooner or later.

I spent my days running simulations on my pod's terminals. The sole function of Des Cartes had become the permutations and combinations of trying to find a scientific solution to humanity's crisis. Eight years worth of simulations had proven one thing, it wasn't an accident that Infringe was lifeless. And it was going to become lifeless again soon unless some miracle occurred.

"Faith," Frederick Ezekiel addressed the people, "it is all we need. No matter how dire the circumstances, God has a plan for all of us. Don't be afraid. Don't be confused. Believe in His plan. And be the best person you can be in this moment."

"Nice crap," my voice had torn through the crowd and silenced the man. "Talk about faith. Talk about God."

His supporters darted towards me but Ezekiel motioned them to stop. It was the first time since the first gathering on Infringe that I had spoken to him directly. First time since the day he had humiliated me, cursed me, condemned me as humanity's biggest mistake.

"Speak, scientist," his voice was firm and deep. "Everyone gets a seat at His table, even you."

"There is no hope for us," I said. "Not today, not ever. I tried to believe that we could survive this place, I tried as long as I could. And I lost everything."

"And you," I continue, "speak about God. You have created a degenerate society, as racist and as corrupt as you are. The strong prey upon the weak, the few hold power over the many. Those who oppose you vanish, and the funny thing is that this place isn't large enough for anyone to vanish. Speak about God, live the high life as you have so far. But this planet will not sustain us for long. And then your religion and your angels will not be there to save us."

"Then why don't *you* save us?"

Ezekiel's eyes were still steeled and angry, but his question conveyed a different emotion altogether.

"You are not the only one who lost everything," he said. "All of us lost our Earth, our people, our friends and families. You have cried about it for years. When do you plan to stop mourning and to do something for this society?"

"I have nothing to offer to *your* society."

"Humanity is my society, Doctor. It is all we have here."

Clarice von Goethe had made her way towards me in the crowd. She held my arm and motioned me to stop arguing.

I went to sleep feeling more empty than the day my wife died, and the day my daughter died. My eyes were heavy, weighed down more by guilt than fatigue. Ezekiel asked me to save us. But if I had the power to do that, I would've done so already. Why did he behave like that?

Memories played in my head on a loop as I fell asleep.

I was pulled out by a choking hand upon my face. I felt a cloth inserted deep in my mouth, gagging me completely. Another piece of cloth was thrown over my face. I was overpowered by no less than five men, who held me and the pieces of clothing over my face.

I thrashed about and struggled, but there was nothing I could do. I couldn't even scream. I felt myself being carried over a slope, and I knew where I was being taken. I felt myself drenched in sweat as the heat rose through my body. I felt a burning sensation near my eyes. It was as if my head was dipped in a furnace. The heat seared and burned my skin, and everything had started to appear red.

Then I heard a gunshot, and I was pulled back to safety.

"Let him be," it was the voice of Frederick Ezekiel. "I need to talk to him."

The Confrontation

A splash of water over my covered face brought me to my senses. The last thing I remembered was Ezekiel's voice asking my unknown assaulters to spare my life. I had passed out almost instantly. I suppose what doesn't kill you makes you pass out. I still felt the terror I had felt when I had nearly been burnt alive.

"I wish we had met in better circumstances. What I am going to talk to you about, it is very crucial. Not only to this world but for you."

My face was uncovered, revealing a pitch-black around me. I was in a dark room. I heard footsteps fade away behind me, suggesting that an exit must be that way. I was not bound in any way, so I could get up and leave any time I wanted. But I felt too weak to get up from the chair I was seated in, so I simply sat there.

"What do you want?"

My feeble question was answered by the sound of something being dragged on the table in front of me.

"I want you to drink."

My hands probed the dark. I found the glass of water that had been offered to me. I was weak, but I drank it up with amazing dexterity.

"I apologize for the inconvenience you had to go through," Ezekiel said. "I had no hand behind it, I assure you."

A flicker of light burnt into existence a couple of meters away from me. In its faint glow, I saw the silhouette of the old, droopy man. He lit a candle, then another, then another, until there was enough illumination around him. Whatever you say about the man, he had a taste for theatrics. His steely eyes looked at me hard, his sharp features threatening to hack me into pieces with nothing but a stare. But his voice was soft and deep, as calm as it would sound in a public sermon.

"How do you feel now?"

"I feel like burning your face with one of your candles, and then ask you how you feel."

Frederick guffawed at my retort, dismissing it from his attention with a shift of stance.

"It seems your retirement came to an end today," he said, "and you finally came up and spoke something in public."

"I was not giving a speech," I said. "I was telling the people how pointless everything is that they are doing, and that you are nothing but a racist fraud. And your supporters just confirmed my suspicions about you. Just wait until I expose you to this *new* world you are so fond of."

Frederick stayed silent for a good minute as if he expected me to speak some more. When he was certain that I had said my piece, he took a deep breath and spoke.

"You have so much going on in your mind. I could take this conversation into so many directions, depending on which of your allegations I choose to discuss. I could tell you that I hate this world as much as you do, and we could talk about that for hours. I could tell you that the supporters of mine you speak of, they simply acted out on their own.

I could also say that you should be careful before you make tall claims about exposing somebody, especially when you just survived death by the hair on your neck. Not a threat, just advice.

But what really intrigues me is your interest in exposing me as a fraud and telling the people that their lives are worth nothing. It begs the question, why are *you* so interested in the workings of this world? You have always believed that you don't give a damn about anything anymore. And yet, you are keenly worried about this world. It's almost laughable."

"I am not," I spoke firmly, "worried about anything. I just..."

The pause was embarrassing. I hated running out of words in the middle of an argument. My wife used to put me in that kind of situation very often, and I had soon realized that I only stammered when a part of me knew that she was right and I wasn't. What if the same was going on with Frederick Ezekiel too?

"I am listening." His calm invocation hit me as an insult.

"I don't care what you believe. I have nothing to prove to you."

"No?" His voice grew deeper and louder. "You don't? But of course, why would you have anything to prove to me? No, it's the people of this world you must answer to. It's the people you must apologize to."

I laughed.

"You have lost it, old man. I have no reason to apologize to anyone."

"Really?" Ezekiel stood up with such force that it made me press myself deeper into my chair. "You don't have anything to apologize for? Such blasphemy! And you call me a fraud."

He approached me, his eyes glittering like a predator's.

"You were a captain," he said, "just like me. Seven captains, charged with the duty to protect the remains of our race and help it reach safely to its destination. Seven captains who were given just one duty. Protect the last of us."

"And you," he pointed his finger at me with hate-filled eyes, "the scientist. You were awake when we came out of hyperspace. You saw this planet. And you knew. You knew what doom awaited us here.

And what did you do about it? What did you do?"

"Frederick, Des Cartes was offline. I couldn't do anything about it."

"Des Cartes was not our captain. You were. You could've taken control of the pods and redirected them. You could've saved all of us."

"There wasn't enough time," I was almost pleading. "My pod was ahead of the fleet, I had to take control of it. My family was in there with me. My wife, my little baby daughter. I couldn't think of anything else."

"Seven billion people had already paid the price for your family," he was shouting now. "You had no right to condemn us all for your family, again. There were fifteen thousand little babies aboard our ship. Twelve made it to Infringe and survived. All because you didn't realize your duty towards humanity. Instead, you saved yourself and your family. You abandoned your entire race."

"Fuck humanity," I said, "and fuck this world. All of us were dead anyway. Even if I had saved all of you and sacrificed my family instead, you wouldn't last five years on this planet. That choice never mattered. Nothing ever mattered since we destroyed Earth."

"Is that what you tell yourself every time you go to sleep?"

A lump formed in my throat. I broke down into tears.

"We are all monsters, scientist," Ezekiel said. "I am a racist, you are a coward. We cannot represent humanity, because we are not humans. We are beneath that, we are subhuman. But we are all humanity has left."

"What do you want me to do?"

"I want you to atone for your sins," he said. "You shirked your duties, and you turned your back on all of us. Now you can continue doing that, or you can wake up and be the captain you were once supposed to be."

I shook my head.

"How do I do that?"

"Save us," he said. "Save humanity."

World Engine

"Des Cartes," I shouted, "where the hell are you?"

It was the third time I was addressing the AI, and again I was met with silence.

"Why do you always vanish when you are needed the most?"

"I am sorry," the automated voice finally echoed through my room, "it has been four years since you addressed me. I had become used to the silence."

"Thank you for the sarcasm," I said. "I have been a lazy prick in the past, I admit it. But you don't need to press the issue."

"I may or may not agree with you, but I never meant sarcasm when I said that I got used to silence."

I opened up the dedicated terminal of the essential remains of my battered life pod, rerouting all simulation data Des Cartes had generated over the years.

"I can't figure out what you are trying to find out in this data," the AI asked.

"Answers," was my reply.

Des Cartes reminded me that these were all failed simulations.

"Have you ever heard of Edison?" I asked.

"Thomas Elva Edison," Des Cartes sounded like a man whose pride was hurt. "The inventor of the incandescent light bulb. He is there in my database."

"Yes," I said. "Do you know how many metals and alloys he tested before Tungsten, the metal that finally made the filament of his light bulb?"

"I don't think that is relevant."

"Over two thousand," I pressed the point. "He tested two thousand metallic substances, alloys, combinations, until Tungsten. One day, when he was still testing and failing, his assistant asked him that since he said that science was a path of constant learning, could he tell what he had learned with his incandescent bulb experiments so far. Edison said - 'I have learned about two thousand metals that cannot be used to make a light bulb.' Failure, you see, is not always the end of the line. Sometimes, it could be the beginning of a new one."

"I still don't see the relevance," Des Cartes said. "What are we trying to find here?"

"Immediate solutions," I said. "Making ourselves completely sustainable may be a long shot, but we can at least solve our immediate problems. The water crisis, for example."

"The water crisis is relatively easy to solve. The conveyor bots could carry ice from the night side and melt it near the dayside. It would keep a fresh supply of water coming. The only problem would be component degradation. And I'm not sure how many bots would be functional today. They have been completely neglected since we landed here."

I pored over the idea with frowned brows. Something struck me as odd.

"Show me the simulation data," I said. "I don't understand. How can this be sustainable? The planet is sterile, and the two hemispheres are practically unconnected. But the simulations show that the ice will not get exhausted. It doesn't make sense, unless..."

I don't know why crazy scientists shouted 'Eureka' when they made a discovery, but I did the same thing that day. I ran through the streets between the columns of houses, chanting the word. I tried to tell people about it, but I was too excited to actually talk. I ended up rushing through the words and making no sense at all.

It was another gathering by Frederick Ezekiel that I unceremoniously interrupted. This time his supporters seemed to be prepared for me, and they grabbed me and started pulling me away even before Frederick could notice me.

"Hey Ezekiel," I shouted at the top of my voice. "I need to talk to you."

I don't know what he saw in my eyes, but he had almost sprinted towards me. Brushing aside the crowd waiting on him, he asked the people to let go of me.

"I need your help," was the first thing I said to him.

"What kind of help?"

"I need all the people who can work," I said, "to help me save this planet."

Des Cartes had been busy, meanwhile. It had already tasked all the bots for taking apart the life pods that had landed on Infringe. The people wouldn't listen to me, but they listened to Frederick Ezekiel and Clarice von Goethe. Once they were told that they were required to help me build a 'world engine' that would bring Infringe back to life, they didn't stop to ask questions.

Soon hundreds of silver lines were laid over our land, lines that went into the cold water and stretched to the icy reaches of the night side at one end, and entered the burning day side of the planet on the other side. I let Des Cartes announce that the 'world engine' was now active, and fourteen thousand cheers filled the sky.

"But you didn't tell us," someone from the crowd asked, "how this 'world engine' works."

"I believe Dr Naik should answer this question," Des Cartes said, "since he is the one who came up with the idea in the first place."

I felt my introvert side grab hold of me while fourteen thousand questioning eyes looked at me with anticipation. What I had achieved was nothing short of a miracle.

"It all started when I was looking through the simulations Des Cartes had done on the possible ways to solve the water crisis," I explained. "I saw that the idea was to bring ice from the night side and melt it down and use it here. That seems right, but the question arises, how long until all the ice is gone?

That was where something funny happened. According to the simulation, the ice would never be gone. Somehow, the planet is capable of replenishing the ice on the night side, it turns out. And there is only one way that can happen."

Amidst the silence, I declared, "the water cycle. This planet has a water cycle of its own. There are no rivers, no proper sea, not even proper temperature and pressure differences to work with. But it has a water cycle.

And that gave me the idea. What if, instead of bringing ice over and melting it down, we bring the heat from the dayside and send it to the night side? The ice would melt, but get replenished. And more ice would melt, and more, and more. For that, I tasked the conveyor bots to collect all the superconductor wirings from the life pods we had available, which you then joined to set up the link between the day and night sides."

"Oh my, that is a genius plan," a female voice arose from the crowd. "Now we have no need to worry about the water crisis."

"That is correct, ma'am," I said, "but this solution is not about solving the water crisis. This solution is about making Infringe inhabitable again."

I didn't need confirmation to continue this time. I already knew that my words were the single most important thing happening on the planet at the time, apart from my world engine working up.

"The superconductors will carry heat from the dayside and send it to the night side, where it will melt the water. Soon, that water will we carried through the silver tubes surrounding the semiconductor wires and reach us. The remaining water will be sent to the higher reaches of the atmosphere by boiling it up at the dayside.

The water vapours shall ionize in the higher atmosphere. Soon, a dense ionosphere shall form over Infringe. This blanket of ions shall capture the heat of the star in the upper atmosphere itself, and spread it evenly around the planet. You can think of the planet being surrounded by a copper mesh. Soon, temperatures around the planet shall equalize.

At the same time, we would be pumping water inside the ground level, into the underground caves that once had the water table of this planet. The water inside shall take the ground heat of the dayside and spread it equitably to the colder side."

"We ran several simulations of this plan," I added, "and we found out that this process will be complete within a year. The average surface temperature of Infringe will be a comfortable twenty-six degrees Celsius, give or take one degree, after a year. Life will thrive all over the planet. And humanity will survive."

The following roar would've shattered the heavens. These were the survivors that had gone through repeated extinctions of the human race within one life. And they had come out as the torch-bearers of the next reign of humanity.

In the distance, somewhere in the crowd, Frederick Ezekiel's steely eyes were fixed upon me. His lips were twisted into a mysterious smile. It was the first time I had seen him smile since our landing. But he still looked at me with hatred. A hatred that burned hotter than the dayside of Infringe, and was icier than the night side of the planet. It was funny. I had saved humanity from imminent destruction, but I couldn't get one stubborn old man to stop hating me.

But then, there's only so much a scientist can do!

Epilogue

"When the light betrays you, trust the darkness. Life may leave you confused, but it will never leave you friendless."

Many might say that our story is tragic. We lost Earth, seven billion people upon it. Then we lost our ship. Then we lost almost all of the crew. The meagre few that remained got stuck on a planet where there was no hope for life, just a time bomb ticking away. I lost my family and everything that I had ever known and loved. Many would say that ours is a story full of negativity.

But I say that our story is more than meets the eye. Sometimes, we need to lose ourselves to find our true purpose. No matter how trivial or routine our struggles are, they are all meant to point us towards our reality.

Clarice von Goethe had been a popular political figure in Germany, Earth. She had a husband and two sons. But they were on a different shuttle, one that landed on the dark side of Infringe. She became a humanitarian after we landed.

Frederick Ezekiel had been a priest, a profession that he continued. He had his fair share of losses too. He was selected for Project Constellation, but his young daughter wasn't. He came aboard the ship knowing her fate, knowing that he had left without saying goodbye, without for once telling her the truth she had always deserved to know.

The only difference between me and them was that I realized my purpose later.

Does that make me a bad person? Or does it make them stronger people than me?

I don't know. I don't want to either. Life happened for all of us the way it was supposed to happen, and we made our choices to the best of our abilities. We all had our roles, and we played them sooner or later.

"The answer is no," Clarice sighed as she closed the old diary. "You were the strongest of us. Because you let us pull you out of the darkness when we needed you."

After all, we are all remembered for our deeds. And that sulking scientist had performed the greatest miracle ever.

"Please keep it safe with you," he had said in his final moments. "I don't want anyone reading it but you."

She had read it every single day. She had a request to fulfil. "When we meet again, not in this world, you better have an answer to all the questions I put in there."

Outside the house at some distance, a young man wiped the sweat off his brow. He had been working hard on the harvest, and it had been a resounding success. It was expected, though. He had his father's intellect for innovation, and he had the last AI of the human race at his aid. The youngster basked in the eternal starlight that lit the dayside, his skin enjoying the mild warmth. He knew where his mother would be.

A smile escaped her lips as Clarice remembered the day when the miracle had occurred.

"What will we call this machine, this world engine, of yours?" She had asked.

"Let's call her Gaia," had been the answer.

Clarice kept the diary in a small pit, freshly dug, besides his tombstone. As she covered it, she laughed.

"You clever bastard," she said. "You set me up on a wild goose chase so that I wouldn't miss you too much. You already knew all these answers."

"We are all lost until we find ourselves," he had often said.

She had been lost since she lost him, all these years. But now, it was time to move on.